I0570597

To my dad

Also By Justin Grimbol

I Still Love You, Peggy Bundy: Poems

Impossible Driveways

Minivan Poems

Mud Season

Come Home, We Love You Still

Hard Bodies

Naked Friends

Drinking Until Morning

The Party Lords

The Creek

The Crud Masters

Bird Castles

Grimboli   Bella

Justin Grimbol

ATLATL

Atlatl Press
POB 521
Dayton, Ohio 45401
atlatlpress.com
info@atlatlpress.com

Bird Castles
Copyright © 2019 by Justin Grimbol
All interior photographs copyright © 2019 by Justin Grimbol
Cover design copyright © 2019 by Squidbar Designs
ISBN-13: 978-1-941918-55-5

This book is a work of fiction. Names, characters, business organizations, places, events, and incidents either are the product of the author's imagination or are used fictitiously. The author's use of names of actual persons (living or dead), places, and characters is incidental to the purposes of the plot, and is not intended to change the entirely fictional character of the work.

No part of this work may be reproduced, stored in a retrieval system, or transmitted by any means without the written permission of the author or publisher.

BIRD CASTLES

BIRD CASTLES

PART

ONE

PART

ONE

ONE

BELLA AND I walked into my old bedroom and put our bags down. I had grown up here. There was proof. As we unpacked we found old stuff. We found stale cigarettes and socks so dirty they looked petrified. We found a porn tape called *Horny Holes, Dripping Poles*. The walls were covered in pieces of scotch tape from where I used to hang posters and flyers for hardcore punk shows. Bella searched through my dresser and found the most precious relic from my past.

"Dear God, what is this?" she said.

"It's my ponytail."

"It's so long," Bella said. "How old is this thing?"

"It's a very old and very fancy ponytail," I said. "I cut it off when I was in the ninth grade. Smell it."

"No way."

"It still smells like Pantene Pro V."

We continued searching.

There were empty bottles of nasal spray and condoms and a pair of panties and a pornographic comic book.

There were pictures of myself naked getting sprayed with silly string by my friend Craig.

"Those were good times," I said.

Bella gave me a suspicious look.

"You can keep this picture," I said. "Do what you want with it."

She laughed.

Her hair was blond and long. It almost reached down to her large butt. I sniffed her romantically.

"How long are we going to live here?" she asked.

"Just the summer. We get rich, then skedaddle."

"This place seems kinda awful."

"It is."

"And expensive."

"Yup."

"And not friendly."

"Might be the least friendly place in the world."

"At least there's a beach nearby," she said.

"Long Beach is less than a mile away."

"Did you go there a lot when you were little?"

"No. Not often. I became moody at a really young age."

"How young?"

"Like nine."

"Jesus."

"Besides, there were too many jellyfish."

"You are such a baby."

I kept sniffing her. I sniffed so hard I made a snorting sound.

She turned to me and smiled.

We kissed. It was a bad kiss. Even though we had been dating for a few years, we hadn't figured out how to kiss each other well. Our kissing style was sloppy and out of sync. It was too moist. There was either too much tongue or not enough tongue. I'd open my mouth and she'd keep hers closed. Sometimes she would open her mouth really wide, but I couldn't find her tongue. She was hiding it somewhere in her gigantic mouth. God only knew where. It was a messy thing. Still, I loved it. So I kissed her long and hard and sloppily. This was it. This was passion. This was romance.

"You need to brush your teeth," she told me.

"No way," I said. "I'm on a diet."

We laughed.

I tried to kiss her again but she dodged away.

TWO

BELLA FOUND A joint while filling my dresser with her clothing. It was a pathetic looking thing. At first she thought it was a toenail. A really big toenail. She hated toenails. But then she looked closer. It was weed. It was the end of an ancient, poorly rolled joint.

We smoked it. Even though we only got a couple drags off the thing it got us really, really stoned and ghostly feeling.

We sat on the floor and leaned against the bed. There was a whole houseful of furniture, stuff my mom had bought while she was still alive, but we preferred to hide out in my room and sit on the floor.

"I want to do stuff," Bella said.

"I want to do stuff, too."

"I want to be active."

"So active."

6

"I want to be a go-getter."

"I want to be like a tiger."

"Grimboli, at first I was kinda sad about having to move into your childhood home for the summer."

"Me too. Too many rich people."

"But now that I'm a little stoned, I realize we can make the best out of this."

"I agree. We can make this summer really fun."

"But we have to be active."

"Very active."

"Like right now."

"Yes."

"I want to go for a run and swim at the fucking beach," Bella said.

I shook my head. That was too much, too active for me.

"Come on, the best part of living in the Hamptons is the beach. Don't take that away from me."

"I'm not. I just don't want to go right now."

"You are such an indoor cat."

"I am not."

"Are too."

"Okay," I said. "I have a better idea. An idea that involves compromise and diplomacy."

She laughed.

"Diplomacy!" she yelled.

"Let's do separate stuff and reconvene," I said.

"Reconvene? Like meet up later?"

"Right. We'll meet up. Maybe have sex. Maybe go for a walk."

"Sounds like a plan."

She ran off to the beach and I stayed behind, starfishing on my bed, scratching my tummy. I felt peaceful for a little while, then I got bored. I decided I wanted to rent some movies. But I also didn't want to come across as lazy, so I made an occasion out of it and dressed up in a button-down shirt and tan slacks. I drove to the 7-Eleven to buy a diet soda. My hometown, Sag Harbor, looked so fancy. Even the 7-Eleven looked fancy. I wondered if it had always been this way and I was just starting to notice. Had Sag Harbor just snorted a bunch of cash up its butt? Everything looked like it had a personal trainer.

Once I purchased my soda, I walked across the way to the Windmill, then I headed to Long Wharf, which juts out into the bay. It was lined with massive yachts. The yachts had always been there. I remember seeing them when I was a kid.

I felt self-conscious. Sure, I had a suit on. But it was a dusty thing from a thrift store. These rich folks could tell. They knew I was a cheap imposter. I found an ATM and pulled out a hundred dollars and placed the money in my breast pocket, some of it sticking out. Now I seemed fancy enough.

I drove home.

Bella was still at the beach. I was lonely.

I sat on the recliner and waited. I wished my dad still lived in the house. I felt homesick for him coming home and sitting on the couch in his panties, with a plate of chips resting on his large belly. I missed listening to him and my mom bicker about adult things. Things like who was going to get coffee from 7-Eleven and when were they going to retire. And did they love each other still? Should we have a TV in the kitchen? Politics. Being too fat. Dieting. Work stuff. Church stuff. Bills. Whose relatives were the most difficult? Should they move? Is this home? Who was the most self-involved and melodramatic? Coffee. Who the hell was going to get the damn coffee?

My father was a minister. For the past five years he had been living in the church manse on Shelter Island, across the harbor. He rented our home out to cousin Carl from my mom's side of the family, who worked at the local middle school as a guidance counselor. Carl was my mom's sister's youngest son. He was a very normal-looking guy. He looked like he would have done really well getting laid in *Little House on the Prairie* times. That is, if those times were more like the show and less of a desperately drooling bloodbath. He looked very naturally wholesome. But not in an alienating way. He also liked to drink. He liked dirty jokes. He liked debating. Recently he had started dating a little bit. He even told me he had put his finger in a girl's butt. Said he went two knuckles deep. There was a quality to Carl that felt timeless, and he fit in here in the Hamptons. To be fair, he would also fit in at a sock hop in the 1950s or milking a cow in the 1800s.

That day Carl found me sitting on a recliner, staring at the TV, dressed in a white button-down and slacks with twenty-dollar bills sticking out of my breast pocket.

"How many hours of *Roseanne* can you watch in one week?" he asked.

"That's what I am trying to figure out," I said.

"Where's Bella?"

"Running."

"You should run with her."

I thought that was funny.

He gave me a long, hard, veiny, disapproving stare down. He didn't approve of the Grimboli tradition of lounging and being lazy and feeling semi-depressed all the time. He wanted me to do stuff. Be active. He didn't care that I was a chubster. He just wanted me to be a fairly physically active chubster.

And I wanted his approval.

"Okay, well, if you aren't going to run with your girlfriend, you can come clamming with me. I'm making pasta with clam sauce for dinner."

"Sounds like fun," I said. "Let's do it."

We drove to a secluded beach in Noyac where you could get away with unlicensed clamming. There was an old bridge covered in faded graffiti and when we stepped onto the beach, hermit crabs scattered back into the sand. There were patches of tall beach grass, bent by the wind.

Carl stood on seashell-covered sand. He had a long rake with a metal basket at the end. He would scrape shallow areas. Sometimes he would catch a clam or two in the basket.

I didn't like this technique. It felt too much like exercise.

When I was young I would occasionally go clamming with my buddy Lewis and his grandfather, Bayman. He was a hunched over old guy with intense muscles who smoked unfiltered Lucky Strike cigarettes. He didn't use any tools. He just walked around, smoking and stomping on the ground. Every so often, he would groan and squat and dig his hand into the damp sand and pull up a large clam. That seemed like real clamming. I didn't like this rake Carl had given me. It was too futuristic. As far as I was concerned, it might as well have been drone warfare. I put the rake down and jumped in the water to hunt with my hands. I was still wearing my button-down and slacks. Carl laughed.

"Get in here," I said. "The water's great."

"I'm good with the rake," he said.

I dove down into the sand and came up with a large clam.

Carl took it and put it in a white pail.

I dove again and found another.

There were many razor clams under the water and sometimes they cut me. My hands were bloody and the salt water stung.

I threw one clam at Carl. It missed and broke open against the bridge.

"Come on. That was a perfectly good clam," he said.

I threw a few more clams against the bridge.

"Grimboli, how about you try putting those clams in the bucket," Carl said.

"I just cooked it the old fashioned way."

"I don't know about that."

"Trust me. This is how cavemen cooked things. They just smashed stuff against rocks. That's what they did."

"I think they used fire."

"Eventually. But at first they just smashed stuff. Now I smash clams to honor all the cavemen we have lost over the years."

I beat on my chest and howled.

I bent over and showed him my ass. I shook it around. I spread it open and let my butthole see the sun and sky and the birds and the warm sand and the water and my cousin standing there shaking his head.

"Okay, that's enough of that," he said.

I sat in the water. I zoned out for a bit. A twenty-dollar bill floated past me. I swam to it. I felt so lucky. Who finds money in the water like this? I laughed. The Hamptons was filled with so many rich people, money just floated around the water like seaweed. What a place.

Then I felt my breast pocket and realized it was my money.

The five twenties in my breast pocket had fallen out.

I swam around for a while looking for the other eighty dollars, but I couldn't find it.

THREE

I TOLD BELLA about the money while we were eating dinner, hoping the delicious clams I had caught with my own hands would make her feel forgiving. Instead she looked at each clam and evaluated how much it had cost us.

"This sucks," she said. "We needed that money."

"We didn't really need it that bad."

"Baby, we came here to save money, not send it off to sea."

"I can't help it," I said. "I'm a reckless guy."

"Eddie, what are we going to do?"

"What do you mean?"

"You lost a bunch of our money."

"Relax. It was only eighty bucks."

"That's a lot."

"It is, but we'll be okay. I'll find a way to earn the money back."

I reached over and took Carl's hand in mine.

"Yes, Eddie?"

"Can I borrow eighty bucks for while?"

"No."

"It was worth a try."

Bella got up and washed her plate and walked back to our room.

"She's pretty upset," Carl said.

"I know, and it's all your fault for taking me clamming."

FOUR

FOR WORK, BELLA and I ran a childcare program out of my father's church. Initially he wanted to name it A Place of Grace. I didn't like that though. Children didn't know what grace was. Besides, it made me feel like a cult leader or like I ran a weird new-age spa.

"Okay, how about we call it My Space?" he said.

"I think that name might be taken," I said.

"Then why don't you come up with something," he said.

"I just want to name it something classic. Something kind of old fashioned."

Eventually Bella and I settled on Fun Squad. The kids loved it and the parents thought it was quirky.

My father's office was cozy. He had couches and a recliner. We hung out there as he worked for a while. We took a nap. He eventually woke us up and kicked us out. He had a counseling appointment with a married couple that hated each other "more than any other married couple" he had ever met before.

"Why don't they get divorced?" I asked.

"'Cause they are in their nineties."

"I guess they're almost to the finish line," I said.

Bella laughed.

"That's adorable," she said.

We headed home.

My father's church was on Shelter Island. It was a small place. There were no bridges connecting it to Sag Harbor. We had to take a ferry. During the summers, they had up to three boats running at a time. We waited in a line of cars for ten minutes or so, then a surly ferry worker directed us onto the boat. On the trip back over Bella and I fought about money. I got mad and got out of the Honda and stood at the side of the boat staring at the brooding clouds and smelling the salt water. Bella came out to join me. We bickered some more. Waves crashed against the ferry and sprayed water on us.

Tall pylons lined the docking area. The ferry bounced into one side then the other. I had never seen a ferry dock smoothly. It always ran into the pylons. Always. Those things had to be so durable. And tall. I wondered how deep the water was there. I wondered how deep the pylons went into the ground to make them so sturdy.

The gate went up and we scrambled back to the car. My

childhood home was close. We rushed to my room so we wouldn't have to argue in front of Carl, but I knew he could hear us anyway.

Eventually I gave in and agreed to make a budget and be more conscious of our spending habits. We spent the afternoon sitting on the stoop in front of my house looking out over our unmown lawn, planning a budget.

Then we immediately broke our budget by getting food at Corner Bar.

I loved Corner Bar. It was one of the few restaurants in Sag Harbor that had not become fancy. It reminded me of the way the town used to look. The ceilings were covered in netting and plastic fish. It was dark in there and smelled of grease and beer. There was a painting on the wall of a bunch of sharks playing poker.

Old grimy men lined the bar. Lisa was our waitress. We had been in the same class growing up. We had never gotten along back then but we were friendly now. She caught us up on all the gossip. Who had become a drunk. Who had gotten divorced. Who had a kid, all that.

The food was still expensive. And our tab was disastrous. Bella was very upset. We fought some more and agreed to reconfigure our budget.

We went to bed early and got up early the next morning to get ready for work.

About ten kids showed up that day. To keep them occupied, I had thrown candy around the graveyard behind the church. They ran around the graves. Some of the graves were really old. They had moss growing from their cracks. Some were large and stood like towers and were owned by wealthy dead people. The kids seemed so comfortable in the graveyard. They focused on the task at hand. They wanted candy. Occasionally they would get distracted by the graves and would stare at them and touch them. They would try and read the dead names with their fingers.

Though they found all the candy within the first five minutes, I let them think there was more. They prowled around for hours for candy that wasn't there. I sat on a grave under an elm tree and enjoyed the shade.

"Ghosts eat here," a little girl named Mandy said, pointing at two graves shaped like tables. "They come out at night and eat massive meals, then sleep through the day."

FIVE

CARL TOOK BELLA and me out to a bar and grill in East Hampton called The Goat. We ordered expensive hoppy beers and got drunk quickly.

"Here's to a rainy summer," I said.

"I won't cheers to that," Bella said. "Where the fuck is Noah's ark when you need it."

"Is that what you call your dad's bank account?" Carl said to me.

"Holy shit, no. But it should be," Bella said.

"I don't even think my dad believes in Noah's ark. He's a minister, but he's way too progressive for the ark. His wife, Patty, believes in the ark though. Holy shit, she believes in that ark so fucking bad."

"Patty is a bit more old fashioned," Carl said.

"So old fashioned, she doesn't even believe in evolution," I said.

"She doesn't?" Bella said.

"She hates it."

"So weird."

"Sometimes I wish I didn't believe in evolution," I said.

"Why?" Carl asked.

"I think the world would feel a bit more like Narnia."

"What the fuck is Narnia?" Bella asked.

"It's a fucking magical land."

"Magic?"

"Yeah. You walk through a fucking wardrobe sometimes and it brings you to a magical land."

"Is this a nerd thing?" she asked.

"I'm not a nerd."

"You have a little bit of nerd in you. In your butthole, I mean. You have a nerd's tiny dick in your butthole."

Carl laughed.

"She got you there," he said.

"Do you really not know what Narnia is? You ever read *The Lion, The Witch and The Wardrobe*?"

She shook her head.

"This is fucked."

On the other side of the bar a young boy was having dinner with his mother. In the middle of the meal she got up to use the bathroom, leaving the boy alone.

The boy stared at the beer, then around the bar. He

reached for it and took a sip.

"You did it!" I yelled.

We applauded him.

He gave us a dirty look.

SIX

THE RAIN CONTINUED through the next day. It made work difficult. Playing games indoors with little kids was chaotic and exhausting, so we brought movies.

It didn't work. The movies were old. It was the stuff I had grown up with. The kids only liked new movies. They looked at movies like *Home Alone* like they were documentaries about the Cold War. I might as well have turned on *Gone With the Wind*. They thought they looked like boring torture devices.

A little girl named Mandy told us about a movie she had seen the night before. It was rated R.

"After so much cool fighting and stuff, they went back to his place and did you don't even wanna know what."

"Gross," another girl said.

"These people were doing you don't even wanna know what

all the time."

That's what she called sex.

"Stop saying you don't even wanna know what," Bella told her.

"I don't know what you are talking about," she said.

Eventually we agreed to watch *The Goonies*, which they enjoyed.

Mandy sat on Bella's lap. The rest of the kids sat on the floor, shunning the massive couch along the wall.

At one point in the movie two of the characters started kissing.

"Oh yeah, that's the stuff," Mandy said. "I bet they are going to do you don't even wanna know what."

SEVEN

MY FRIEND CRAIG lived in Brooklyn and made a living doing freelance graphic design. During the summer he moved back to Sag Harbor and designed a fancy magazine called *Nox Hampton*, based out of East Hampton.

The magazine had a large staff that worked hard all day and went out drinking at night. They spent lots of money when they went out and Craig liked to call and tell me stories.

"This guy peed in my boss's pool," Craig told me over the phone. "My boss could tell somehow. He jumped in the pool with all his clothing on and slapped the shit out of the kid. Grimboli, my boss is a bad man."

"Craig, this sounds like the best time ever. You have to bring us along," I said.

"My boss loves throwing money away. He spends so much money. One time he paid a bouncer to let him hang out in a club shirtless. Gave the dude two hundred bucks."

"Is your boss really skinny or fat?"

"He's fat like you."

"Dude."

"Sorry, Grimboli."

"It's okay."

"You really would get a kick out of this guy though. I mean, shit, you should have seen that motherfucker in that club, titties out, jiggling his fat around. Rubbing liquor into his skin like it was suntan lotion. People started licking his body. Strangers just went up to him and licked his belly and nips. He seemed completely unfazed."

One night we met Craig and his friends in a restaurant called World Pie. After the stories I'd been told, I thought hanging out with *Nox* people would be really wild, like ancient Roman times. I figured everyone would be drunk and laughing hard and hatefully, as if they were about to fall on top of each other and break out into an orgy. I had overestimated their partying abilities though. There was no real wildness in them. No orgies. We just sat in a crowded restaurant and barely talked. Craig and his coworkers drank expensive drinks and texted on their phones. Sometimes they took pictures of themselves. That was about as wild as they got. And there wasn't much conversation. They barely acknowledged us.

Craig could tell we were bored. He promised that things

would pick up. Things would get wild.

"Look at my friend," Craig said.

He pointed to a blond kid. The kid didn't look up from his cellphone.

"We call him Prince Valiant 'cause he had this long blond hair. He cut it though. Now he looks like Hillary Clinton."

The kid finally looked up and gave him a snotty look.

"Don't let him tease you," I said to the kid. "Craig wore whatever his parents bought up until he was like twenty years old."

"Those outfits were awesome," Craig said. "I miss my jean shorts."

"I don't care," the kid said.

"Eddie hasn't washed his clothing for over two weeks," Bella said.

"But you love that," Craig said to her. "You love this big man's dirty pants."

"I like it so much," Bella said. "It's awful. I have a weird fetish for men who look like they are having a nervous breakdown. I'm surprised he isn't wearing sweatpants right now."

The restaurant became even more packed.

"I'm tired," Bella said.

I knew that meant I had to get her home. Once Bella said she was tired, it wasn't long before she fell asleep. It would take me forever to wake her up.

Craig tried to convince me to hang out longer. I told him

we would meet up some other time. We had the whole summer ahead of us.

We hugged and Craig paid for our cab even though we only
had a few drinks each and could have driven ourselves home.

EIGHT

THERE WAS A series of intense storms. The kids in our program loved them. We hid in the church and told ghost stories. We played hide and seek. We hung out in the chapel. They took turns pretending to be ministers.

One night we made gingerbread houses. The kids loved the idea of doing something Christmassy in the summertime.

Mandy built the biggest house, but then she smashed it with her little fists.

We thought she was upset but then she looked at us with a boogery smile.

"We should have a sleepover," she said.

"I don't think so," I said.

"Why?"

"'Cause I actually like to sleep," I said.

"We'll let you sleep," the kid said.

I shook my head.

"Come on, I'll make you a special bed. I'll make you a bed made out of Heineken."

I laughed.

I needed to change the subject fast, so I pretended to be a man-beast. I told the kids to pretend to be monsters. I told them to be gross and hungry and vicious. Then I told them to demolish and eat their gingerbread houses.

They stomped around and growled and ate their houses.

One girl didn't like the game and cried and screamed. Bella took her to the chapel and worked on calming her down while I continued to stomp around with the rest of the group.

The parents came to pick up their kids, and we stuck around to pick up the mess. The ferry ride home was rough. Waves burst against the side of the boat. I had to turn my windshield wipers on. Bella loved every minute of it.

"Isn't this exciting?" she kept saying.

NINE

CRAIG CALLED ONE morning sounding very upset. His buddy Calvin had just gotten fired. He had worked with Calvin for years. They had met while working on a different magazine called *Sand in Your Shoes* before it folded and they got the job at *Nox Hampton* together.

Calvin was much older. He had been in the industry before they used computers, but he was still a wild party animal and Craig loved getting drunk with him and talking shit.

"It's so fucked up, Grimboli," Craig told me. "They canned him. They just fucking fired the dude 'cause he had been fucking around too much. After he got fired, he came into my office. The guy got on his knees and begged me to help him. He was crying really hard."

"What did you say?" I asked.

"Not much. I just listened to him. Told him he could find

another job. He kept crying and yelling 'How can they do this to me?' I thought about slapping him. In like, a loving fatherly way. But I didn't."

"That's probably for the best."

I lay in bed and listened. I didn't know how to relate to any of this. It seemed brutal. I had never had a job like that. I had many jobs, but usually when I got fired I felt nothing but relief.

"You want to hang out tonight?" I asked him.

"No, the next issue comes out tomorrow. I have to pull an all-nighter."

"Shit, man. Well, good luck."

"Thanks, Grimboli."

TEN

BELLA WENT FOR a run. She came back an hour later, red faced and sweaty.

I grabbed her and kissed her warm cheeks.

Then I pulled down her running shorts and licked her sweaty butt.

Sex happened. It was sweaty and stinky.

We headed to town and went for a walk and tried to enjoy the cool night. We walked by a place called The Piggy. It was fancy, and the inside looked dark and fragile.

"Why is it called Piggy?" Bella asked.

"It used to be a diner. Like a normal diner. It was filled with piggy banks. They were everywhere."

"Weird."

"It was my mom's favorite place."

"What happened to it?"

"Someone bought it and made it fancier. It was still a diner but the piggy banks were gone. That place shut down for a while. Then someone else bought it. Made it even fancier."

"Did your mom still go to it even though it was fancy?"

"No. She started hanging out at the deli across the street."

"The Golden Pair?"

"No. Oh god no. It was different back then. It was just called The Sag Harbor Deli. She would meet these old dudes. She met them for coffee every morning. If she didn't show up, they called the house."

"What do you mean?"

"One time my mom was sick and she slept in. One of the old dudes from the deli called. I told the dude she was sick. He didn't care. He insisted I wake her up."

"Then what happened?"

"She went to the deli."

"No."

"Yeah, she got up and got dressed and went to the deli to drink coffee with the old men."

"Were they members of her church?"

"Nope."

"And she didn't care?"

"I guess not," I said.

"Was the food at the deli good?"

"I can't remember."

"Which one of these places have you worked at? Didn't you

say you were a bus boy once?"

"I worked here, at The Piggy."

"No shit."

"I was a bus boy."

"How did that go?" she asked.

"Badly."

"How badly?"

"It was rough."

"Tell me more. I want to hear all about it."

"I got demoted."

"Stop."

"I did. I got demoted."

"From a bus boy?"

"Yup. I got demoted to bus boy helper."

She laughed. Then we continued walking. Town was busy, and everybody looked like they were pretending to be models. My poor hometown had become a runway show.

"Why didn't they just fire you?" Bella asked.

"I don't think a town can just fire you from living there," I said.

"No. What? I'm talking about The Piggy. Why didn't they just fire you from The Piggy?"

"Oh. The owners knew my mom. They went to our church. I think she counseled one of them. Or something like that."

ELEVEN

IT RAINED OFF and on. The kids were bored of being inside, so we decided to let them play in the rain.

We chased them around the graveyard pretending to be rain monsters. They loved it. A few of the parents loved it too, but only a few. The rest were confused by the decision. They yelled at their kids for getting wet. They acted as if the children had snuck out into the rain. They knew we had let them out, but the parents yelled at them anyway. The parents just didn't know how else to act.

My father's manse was down the road from the church. His wife, Patty, had been sick for years. She spent most of her time trying not to move much and worrying about the groceries. As soon as we got there she sent us out to buy milk.

It had stopped raining for a bit, so after we got the milk, we took our time walking back. When we got home my father and Patty were sitting on matching recliners, arguing about finances. Patty had a look on her face. It was a look that probably took her most of her life to perfect. It was equal parts tragic and stubborn and pitiful. We sat and listened to them fight for a while. Eventually my father got up and stomped off to his office upstairs. Patty couldn't get up the stairs, even on her best day.

I walked up to the office to check on my dad. He sat at his computer, typing. I hoped he was writing again. He had been longing to start a new book. But when I looked over his shoulder I saw that he was working on a schedule. My father kept meticulous schedules. Sometimes he would plan them years into the future. The thing is he never actually followed them. Tomorrow would come and the old man was going to ignore the schedule he had written. This meant he would have to write more, adjusted schedules. It didn't matter. They were pointless. He just liked to write them.

I asked how he was doing.

"Patty can just drive me crazy," he said.

"I know. She can be a little stubborn."

"A little? She wants to keep the books, but she is on all these meds and she forgets things, so we are months behind on bills. And I just want to scream. Oh well, I'll take care of it. It's a good life if you don't weaken."

He asked about my summer and the program. I told him about the rain monsters and the angry parents and he thought the whole story was adorable and sweet.

Then he asked about Craig. I told him about some of the wild adventures. He only laughed once, and it didn't sound sincere.

"I'm worried about that boy," he said.

"He's fine. He's just being Craig. That's all."

"I guess. Just . . . I think all this drinking can't be good."

"He's having a good time."

"Maybe."

He went back to working on his schedule.

TWELVE

I WAS WORRIED about my father. He seemed too worn out and like he was gaining weight. I started visiting more regularly. Usually Bella and I stopped by his place after work. One night we decided to watch a movie.

"Nothing depressing, okay?" Patty asked.

She gave him a pouty look.

My father nodded and put on a movie about the holocaust.

By the end of the film, Patty was crying uncontrollably.

"No more sad movies," she kept saying. "Only happy movies."

We stuck around a while after the movie. My father went to his office to get some work done.

Bella and I watched TV with Patty. She was still crying but not as intensely.

She put her favorite shopping channel on and started to

cheer up a bit.

We watched TV with her. I felt bored, but cozy.

Patty tried to readjust herself. She had been sitting on the recliner for a long, long time. I couldn't imagine how uncomfortable it got. She moved her arm the wrong way and cried out in pain.

"You okay?" Bella asked.

"I'm fine."

"You sure?"

"I'm sure."

"Can I get you anything?" Bella asked.

Patty thought for a moment. She put her finger to her dried lips.

"No, I'm fine. Really, I'm fine. It's just this rotten disease. But I believe in miracles. One day I will be better. Just you wait and see."

We tried convincing Patty to smoke weed. We told her it would help. She had never smoked weed. She was scared of it.

"I get high on life," she insisted.

"It's different," I said. "It's a different thing entirely."

"But what if I get too doped up and I think I can fly and I try to jump off the roof."

"How would you get to the roof?" Bella asked.

"That's a good question."

We laughed and kept trying to convince her to smoke weed. She refused.

Eventually Patty started falling asleep. Her eyes would lock on the TV. She'd watch the shopping network like it was a list of people who have been found dead in some natural disaster. Her eyes would water. Then shut. She'd sleep for a bit. Then she would wake up and focus on the TV again.

Bella and I walked out to the front porch. Another storm was coming in. We smoked a little weed and watched the clouds in the distance. There would be a flash of light and the rumbling of thunder.

I drank a diet soda and Bella smoked more weed.

Patty had woken up fully now. We could hear her calling out to my father. She needed more milk. My father wouldn't respond.

"We should have sex when we get home," Bella said.

"Stinky sex," I said.

"Our sex is always stinky," she said. "Even if we shower first."

THIRTEEN

CARL MET A woman named Robin. She was a redheaded local who always looked like she had just gotten back from the
gym. She was energetic and fit. She worked at a local vineyard. He took us there for a free tasting. His new girlfriend
was very energetic and informative and explained the taste of
the wine and how it was made. As she talked it was obvious
that she had trouble standing there and not exercising. She
wanted to be doing jumping jacks or something like that. I
enjoyed this about her. I was often bothered by energetic people, but she felt refreshing. She lightened the mood.

I could tell Bella liked it too. We both got drunk and started goofing around.

"This place needs music," I said. "Something that would
make you feel old and rich. Maybe the *Legends of the Fall*
soundtrack."

"Oh God no," Bella said. "Every time Eddie listens to that soundtrack he starts crying."

She laughed and kissed me.

"Or maybe there could be some sexy saxophone music or something like that."

"Is sexy saxophone music a genre?" Carl asked.

His new girlfriend smiled and continued to discuss the wine. There were other customers attending the tasting, other people she had to attend to.

Finally the tour ended and we continued to drink wine, treating the vineyard like a bar. Robin was chill. She liked to drink and bullshit and was trying hard to enjoy us.

"Imagine if this place was a nudist colony. This place would make an amazing nudist colony," I said.

"You can do that if you want. I won't stop you," Robin said.

Bella got really excited.

"Don't encourage them," Carl said.

My cell phone rang. It was Craig. He was also drunk.

I put him on speakerphone.

"Eddie, I'm in Montauk!" he yelled. "I just went to second base with a stranger. Her boobs were pointy. I tried to get milk out of them like I'm a little baby. But I'm not a baby. I'm too old for milk. She didn't mind. She liked it. Then I took a nap and I woke up and second based it again, but then I realized it was a different stranger. A better stranger. Knowwhatimsaying?"

"I love hooking up with strangers," I said.

Bella hit me in the arm.

"I wish you were a stranger," Bella said.

Bella and Robin high-fived.

"Eddie, you need to get down here."

"Can't. Drunk."

"Eddie Grimboli! Craig is a star! You should see me, Eddie. I got a fucking beach body. All day long, baby. Women love this thing. They can't help it. They were born to love my beach body. I'll let them watch it a little."

"Who is that?" Robin said.

She sounded unamused. Disgusted even.

"Who are you?" Craig yelled. "Oh shit? Grimboli, is that Chris? Does she still look all hot and good?"

Things got quiet. Chris was Carl's ex-wife and I could tell by the look on Robin's face she knew that.

Carl didn't look embarrassed. But I could tell he was upset so I hung up the phone on Craig.

There was a long awkward silence, the kind that makes my throat feel tight and my skin itch.

"So," I said. "This wine tastes really oaky. Which is good, right?"

FOURTEEN

CARL AND ROBIN became serious quickly, which meant Carl wasn't around as much. Bella and I had the house to ourselves more often, so we started walking around the house naked and having kinkier sex.

Usually it involved butt play and gymnastics. Once Carl came home and found me naked on the kitchen table with my legs spread open, looking like a stuffed turkey.

He winced and laughed, then begged me to be a bit more discreet. He didn't want Robin coming over and finding me naked and doing stuff.

One afternoon we pissed on each other. Bella stood in the bathtub. I had a boner. I pissed on her. She laughed. She thought it tickled.

Then it was my turn. Being a man of leisure, I lay down in the tub when it was my turn. She pissed on me and I felt completely overwhelmed. It was so hot and thick.

"It's too much!" I yelled.

After that we took a shower. We made some dinner, pasta and a salad. We spread butter on rolls.

After dinner we went for a walk. I showed Bella Pebble Beach. We walked down the shoreline and passed massive mansions with elaborate hedges and marble statues and pools, even though the ocean was right there. One house had two pools.

"Why are these places so empty?" Bella asked.

"Nobody really lives in them. They're summer homes."

"But it's summer."

"Good point."

"So why aren't they here?"

"At a different summer home somewhere."

"You still smell like pee," she said.

"Really? I showered twice."

"One was a piss shower."

"Still counts."

FIFTEEN

MY FATHER TOOK Bella and me for a drive around Shelter Island.

"It's so beautiful here," Bella said.

"There are lots of beaches."

"I love beaches. Eddie baby, why don't you like beaches?"

"I like beaches."

"No you don't."

"I do too."

"You never want to go."

"That's because I don't want to be controlled every second of my life."

"Calm down. You can be so ridiculous sometimes."

"We went to Pebble Beach a couple nights ago."

"That was nice."

"I know."

"We should do that more often."

"You should take the kids to the beach," my dad said.

"I don't know. The weather has been really unpredictable."

"It has been kind of lousy weather," he said.

"How's Patty?" I asked.

"Not good. In a lot of pain."

"How are you?" Bella asked.

"Tired. Wish I could just get up and leave sometimes. Well, most of the time actually."

We continued driving.

Bella didn't find driving to be relaxing. She felt claustrophobic, so my father pulled over and let her go for a walk on the beach.

It was raining and my father was concerned.

"Hope she heads back here soon," he said.

"She'll be fine," I said.

"Eddie, it's raining. She could catch pneumonia."

"You are so paranoid," I said.

He gave me a look that told me I was being insolent and stubborn. We bickered about her health until she finally returned. She was soaking and she was laughing.

"It was nice out there. I went for a swim."

"You did?" my dad said.

He sounded shocked and amused.

"The water was so, so nice."

We drove back to his house and helped Patty with dinner.

She couldn't really move so she just told us what to do. I wasn't very helpful so eventually Bella kicked me out of the kitchen. Patty and I watched some TV and Bella made us spaghetti and meatballs.

She added garlic. Patty didn't tell her to add garlic, but Bella did it anyway. It added some spirit to the meal, but my father was old and big and his stomach didn't handle garlic well. He sat in the living room in his nightgown, the plate of food resting on his large belly, burping up rancid air.

"Bill, stop eating that garlicky sauce," Patty kept saying. "It will upset your tummy."

"I'm fine," he said.

"But your tummy."

"My tummy is fine."

He belched again. It smelled sour and upsetting.

Patty gagged.

"Bill, you are so gassy," she said. "Your poor tummy."

Bella apologized and left the room to get some fresh air.

"This spaghetti is delicious!" my dad called out to Bella. "I love it."

He belched again.

The smell was overpowering. I went outside to join Bella.

Once we came back in, Patty was asleep in her recliner and my dad was upstairs in his office. I could hear him belching.

We cleaned a bit. Did the dishes and folded some of their laundry. Then we drove to the ferry. Usually we used the ferry ticket provided by the church, but we had run out so we had to pay the expensive fee out of pocket. Bella and I bickered about finances all night and had sex in a couple of positions. Turtle style. Then some hetero scissoring.

SIXTEEN

OUR CHILDCARE CENTER was doing well. We didn't have much. We had almost no supplies and we looked like cretins. But we got a lot of kids. To celebrate, Bella and I went to a new restaurant that was supposed to have good Indian food. We split a bowl of curry and only had a few beers, but our bill was still huge. It cost us forty dollars and we were both still hungry by the end of the meal. The whole thing put me in a foul mood.

"Let's get the fuck out of this hellhole," I said.

Bella got mad.

"Stop being so impatient," she said. "I'm still drinking my beer."

"You drink so slowly. You drink it like it's fucking tea. You take these little tiny sips. That's not how you are supposed to drink beer."

"Don't tell me how to drink beer. God, you are so controlling."

"I'm not controlling. It's a known fact of life. You are supposed to drink beer quickly. That's how you get a buzz. How the fuck do you even get a buzz drinking it like that?"

"Will you fuck off please?"

I apologized. Bella loved it when I apologized. Her mood improved drastically. It felt like the night had been redeemed. There was a chance for some romance.

"Tell me what the sexiest thing about me is," she said.

"Your facial expressions," I said.

"Are you fucking serious right now?"

I nodded.

"You are such an asshole."

She wanted me to talk about her ass or her boobs or her eyes or something like that. And I loved those things. She had lots of sexy stuff about her. But I loved her facial expressions more and I was really stubborn about being honest when it came to sex stuff.

"What the fuck!"

I laughed.

"Sorry, but it's true."

"You are such a dick."

"Am not."

"Are too."

"Bella, come on. I was just being honest. Stop being insecure."

"Are you kidding me right now?"

We argued for a while. She didn't blink much. Her eyes looked amazing. I wanted to change my answer. But I didn't. I wanted to win the fight.

That wasn't possible though. She was too angry. I couldn't understand why.

Eventually, we headed home.

It rained again that night. There had been so many storms. It seemed strange.

We drank more and I apologized and told her how nice her eyes were and how nice her pussy felt. That cheered her up. It also made her want to fuck. I didn't like fucking when I was drunk. My sex stuff spent its sober time in overdrive. Constantly pressed against pants and dripping and needy. I had a teenage pecker when I was sober. It was my mini-horse and it needed to Zen-out sometimes. It needed to be an old man weeny. Also, I didn't see the point. Usually drunk sex was fun because it lowered inhibition. Bella had no inhibition when she was sober. She was actually a bit more finicky when drunk. She was also clumsy. Usually drunk sex involved her stepping on my wiener at least once.

We argued about that for a while. We argued until we were exhausted and went to sleep.

I woke up in the middle of the night delirious and horny. I fondled her boobs. We had sex.

SEVENTEEN

CRAIG CALLED WHILE I was at work. I had kids hanging off me like I was a jungle gym.

"Eddie, man, I went a little too wild last night."

"What happened?"

"I was ready for a good night. But my buddy who looks like Hillary Clinton wanted to go home early. I got mad. Lectured him about loyalty. Then I punched him in the face. Then I fired him."

"You can fire people?"

"Of course. I'm in charge of design. I'm the boss of this shit. I might have to hire him back though."

The kids from our program were screaming and being loud.

"Eddie, what the fuck is going on over there?" Craig asked.

"Just working."

"Babysitting sounds difficult."

"It is. Can I call you back later?"

"Of course. Later, man."

I hung up and gathered the kids.

"New game!" I yelled. "Everyone tickle Bella!"

They swarmed Bella. She screamed and laughed and begged for mercy.

After work we headed home. The weather was stormy, making the ride on the ferry rough and anxiety producing.

When we got home I found a message written for me by Carl. It said that someone from my mom's old church had called. There was a number. I hadn't heard from anyone from that church in a long time. Since my mom passed they had gone through a number of ministers. Most of them were awkward and short-lived, and membership had declined.

I called the number. Mr. Carlton answered. He invited me to the church the next day. He said they had a gift to give me. I thought that was strange.

"What do you think it is?" Bella asked.

"I don't know. Maybe money."

"Why would they give you money?"

"'Cause I'm so sad."

"You aren't that sad."

"I get sad."

"Come on. Why do you really think they called?" Bella asked.

"No clue."

EIGHTEEN

BELLA OFFERED TO drive me, but I wanted to walk. It was a nice day. Windy and no rain. Not too hot. I headed down Route 114. I passed by Newman's Boat Parts. I had walked by it hundreds of times when I was young, but I had never been inside. What if it was amazing in there? What if there were french fries in there? What if they sold french fries and boat parts this whole time and I had no idea? *I should go in there*, I thought. *I should go in there just once.* I walked by, as I always had.

I took my time over the bridge and even made sure to spit onto a passing boat the way I used to when I was young. I bought myself a diet soda at 7-Eleven.

Town was swarming with rich, attractive people. They all looked so let down. The worst part of living in a tourist town was how disappointed the tourists always seemed, even though it was their presence, their traffic, and their expensive habits that made the place disappointing.

I took a left at the end of Main Street. I walked by the old historic fire department to the Old Whaler's Church.

It was a strange-looking place. It looked like a fortress painted picket fence white. The church's steeple was gone. The church used to have one. A really big one. It was almost two hundred feet tall, and whalers could see it all the way from Montauk Point. It told them they were almost home.

The town was heartbroken when winds from a hurricane lifted it off and dumped it onto the street.

People talked about replacing the steeple for all of the ten years my mom preached there. It never happened. Probably never would.

I walked up the blue stairs that led to the large doors. I opened them and saw Mr. Carlton standing in the vestry. We shook hands. He looked so old. But then again, he always had.

Mr. Carlton walked with me around the church. It smelled dusty and familiar.

He told me about the restorations. They had put in new windows. Now the sanctuary got more light. They had taken down one of the stained-glass windowpanes and framed it. He told me it would go to me, and I thanked him for the gift.

We sat on one of the pews. He asked how I was doing. I told him about my girlfriend and the house and my cousin. My father had remarried but his wife was sick.

Mr. Carlton used to teach Sunday school. He asked about my old Sunday school class.

"Have you seen any of those folks?" he asked.

"Sure, Lisa works at Corner Bar."

"How's she?"

"Can't tell. Okay, I guess."

His eyes started to fill with tears.

I tried to think of something to say. I felt like a kid. Staring at a computer. Trying to write a book report. Not having a clue what to write about a book I have not read.

"I miss your mother," he told me.

I sat with the guy for a while. Then I headed out. The wind had picked up and I felt peaceful. I walked around for a while. I got dinner at Concadorro's Pizza. I ordered a couple slices. Then ordered a couple more.

Bella called.

"I want to party," I told her. "I want to drink."

"Sounds like fun," she said.

"I want to dance."

"Let's do it."

A couple hours later Carl, Robin and Bella met me at Murf's Pub. The bar looked old and cozy but most of the customers were dressed up like they were born on a yacht and raised on leather couches, lobster tails and drinking champagne. They looked like this was their first time on land and they were really excited to drink beer for the first time.

Bella and I got drunk quickly. It was a rowdy night. There was lots of yelling and bad jokes and laughter. It seemed like the kind of night that would keep us going. Eventually we'd all be getting lunch together. We'd eat egg sandwiches at the Bagel Buoy and feed the scraps to seagulls. Maybe nudity would happen. And not normal-relationship nudity. Stumble-down-the-streets-with-your-pants-around-your-ankles nudity. That spiritual nudity where you spread your butt cheeks at strangers as if they were your doctor. That kind of nudity.

I gave Carl lots of hugs. I told him I loved him. I told him his new girlfriend was beautiful. She had a butt that made me emotional. So much power there. So much pale, curvy, bicycle peddling, gym membership power.

I gave her a long hug.

"You have a really interesting smell," she told me.

"I'm all natural."

"It's almost too natural," she said.

I gave another round of hugs.

Then I had to go to the bathroom. The toilet in the bar was filled to the brim with toilet paper. I squatted over it and pooped.

I was expecting it to be such a productive session. I felt bad leaving the mound there, simmering, so I tried to flush it.

The toilet filled with water and started to overflow. Slimy toilet water covered the floor. There was so much of it. I felt like I was in a sinking ship.

The water flooded out of the bathroom and into the bar.

I could hear women screaming.

I stood in the bathroom and considered my options. Something had to be done. I was going to flood the entire town at this rate. Or at least the bar.

Right as I was about to stick my arm into the toilet, the bartender kicked open the door.

"I don't know what happened," I said. "I was just taking a little tinkle and then the toilet just started acting all weird and demonic and shit."

He told me to leave.

I ran out of the bar. Rich ladies pinched their noses as I passed.

"Bella!" I yelled.

"Dude, I'm right here," she said.

I told her what had happened. I thought she was going to be angry. Instead she started laughing.

"You dumb shit," she said.

Carl wasn't as amused. He listed all the other places in town I could have gone to the bathroom. None of these places were very far away.

When we got home, I changed my outfit. Then I tried to get everyone riled up and ready for more drinking. But Carl had gone to Robin's place for the night.

"Let's just party, the two of us," Bella said.

"I don't want to party with just you," I said.

"Why not?"

"Partying alone with your girlfriend is boring."

"What the hell is wrong with you?"

"I'm just being honest."

"You are just being an asshole."

"Okay fine. Let's drink."

"No. I'm just going to shower and go to bed."

She undressed and I tried to grab her butt. She slapped my hand away.

She walked off and I looked through my dresser for an old porn tape or maybe a comic or something. I ended up finding an old pack of cigarettes. Camel Lights. They smelled stale.

I sat out on the front stoop and smoked. It made me light headed.

Once I finished, I flicked the cigarette butt into the driveway and stumbled back into the house to bed.

NINETEEN

"I NEED A friend," I said. "I need a friend with benefits."

"Stop being so annoying!" Bella yelled.

She tried to push me into the water. We were walking down a long beach. The sky looked moody. There had been so many storms.

"I just really want a mistress," I said. "Someone different."

I laughed and stuck my tongue out at her.

"Fuck off. You ever think that maybe I want a guy whose balls don't smell so bad?"

"I want a woman who smells like balls."

"So gross."

I looked up at the sky.

"What if there's a tornado?" I said.

"Stop. Long Island doesn't get tornados."

"We live in strange times. Pollution. Global warming. We

could get a tornado."

She shook her head.

"I sure hope I get to have group sex one day."

"You need to stop with that," she said.

"Holy shit, I just realized something."

"What?"

"We're going for a long leisurely walk on the beach. We're fucking romantic."

"We really are," she said.

TWENTY

THE STORMS BECAME less frequent. I got my first sunburn. Bella spent even more time running on the beach while I stayed home watching *Roseanne*.

Our childcare program became busier. Sometimes we would get up to thirty kids. It was too much. We tried hiring some teenagers from my father's youth group, but most of them just hung out on the playground and rarely lifted a finger to assist us. One even fell asleep under the picnic table. He slept through the entire day's program. We let the kids draw on his face. At the end of the day we left him to sleep and went home.

Bella felt burnt out. We worked Monday through Saturday. On Sunday, we went to church to see my father preach. Bella counted this as a day at work. I didn't think going to church was work. It was not fun, but it was not really working either.

We fought about this frequently. One Sunday I decided we should skip church and relax. We went to the ocean. The waves were tall and loud. Fancy people stood in the breaking water and got knocked over. There were people in thongs. So many thongs. So many butts. Bella brought wine. This was her day off. No old church ladies. No hymns. No stale finger foods for coffee hour. Just waves and butts and wine and the heat from the sun.

Craig called. I told him to join us.

"Don't know if I can deal with all that sand," he said.

"Come on, dude."

"I guess I should come. I don't want to let the whole summer pass by without having gone to the ocean at least once."

I was amazed by how quickly Craig got to the beach.

"I drive really fast," he said.

He looked over at Bella and laughed.

"Bella, your boobs are out," he said.

She rolled over, laughed, and shook her boobs at us.

"Release the twins!" she yelled.

"And you're drunk," Craig said. "That's cool."

"It's my day off and I decided to not be responsible in any way. Get into it!"

"Too hungover and sad," Craig said. "Deep sad. Talked to the ex."

"You have an ex?"

"Rich Mexican."

"She's very beautiful," I said. "They met in New York. So rich. I've never seen her smile."

"She smiles," Craig said. "I saw her smile a lot."

"That's good."

"How did you meet her?" Bella asked.

I laughed. Then I stretched out on the sand like a beached whale. I had heard this story many times. It was a long story, and Craig really took his time telling it.

He went over all the main events. How they met. Their long, sloppy courting. All the drinking and fights and epic sex. Falling in love. Dating. Lavish restaurants. Thousand-dollar meals. Her family in Mexico. Her wealth. The intimidating father. Her brothers loving Craig. Lots of drinking. But the money was too much, and the standards were impossible. So many restaurants. Craig hated restaurants. He preferred peanut butter sandwiches. The fights were brutal. She could be cold. There were so many fights. He ranted on and on, about all their break-ups and all the times he won her back. All their fights.

Now she lived in Florida. This made their most recent breakup feel more permanent than the others. He missed her.

"The thing is," he explained. "I grew up with my parents having this perfect marriage. They met young. Got married. Have had a happy marriage. They are traditional. I was wired to meet one woman and fall in love and be a provider. That's the Craig way. But I'm glitchy. I keep getting into these dysfunctional relationships."

Bella had fallen asleep toward the end of the story. Craig didn't seem offended.

"She looks happy," he said.

"She likes the sun," I said.

We watched the ocean. The waves were still big from the storms. People stood as close as they could and let the waves knock them around. Sometimes this looked really silly to me. Sometimes it seemed pathetic. Right then they looked almost like they were praying, and each time a wave crashed into them and knocked them down, it was a prayer answered.

TWENTY-ONE

EVENTUALLY WE GOT bored and woke Bella. This was not easy. Bella loved to nap and hated being woken up. She rolled around the warm sand and groaned and slapped my hand away.

"Come on, baby," I said. "Let's go."

I nudged her more aggressively.

She lashed out and tried to kick me. She had thick strong legs.

"Fuck off," she said.

"Please!" I yelled. "Don't do this! The beach is too hot! Too sandy!"

Craig laughed.

"Should we just drag her to the car?" he said.

"Maybe."

We grabbed her feet. She started kicking. She got me in

the stomach. I fell over.

"What the fuck, Bella?"

"Fuck you, Eddie!"

She kept her eyes shut. Even when she yelled, her eyes were sealed shut.

"What the hell is your problem?" I yelled.

"What's your problem?"

"You're acting like a child."

"No. You are."

I tried to grab her foot again. She kicked me in the chest.

I screamed.

"You guys doing okay?" Craig asked.

"Yes. We're fine."

Craig knelt down and started rolling Bella like a log. She groaned. He kept rolling her. She tried to roll back. She tried to roll the other direction. It didn't work. Craig was strong. She gave up. She started laughing.

She stood up. She still looked tired.

Once she was in the car she passed out in the backseat. We followed Craig back to his place. During the year, he lived in the city working as a freelance designer. The magazine was a summertime gig. While working for *Nox Hampton* he stayed with his parents. I had forgotten this. For most of the summer I imagined him living a lush lifestyle. Nothing but fanciness. But this wasn't the case. He slept at home in his childhood bed. He ate breakfast with his parents in the morning.

Scrambled eggs. Bacon. Toast. Orange juice.

Bella wanted to nap in the car, so we left her there.

Craig and I had some milk and oatmeal cookies. His parents' pantry always had some cookies. Then we went to the basement where we used to play video games. The consoles were no longer there, but the TV was and there were two old recliners set up in front of a large flat screen just like when we were young.

We sat and looked at the blank screen.

One of his old art school paintings leaned against the couch.

"You ever think about painting anymore?" I asked him. "I miss your paintings."

"No."

"Why not?"

"Not enough time."

"I can see that."

"Craig has to go all in. If I was going to paint I would only be able to do it here and there. Like a hobby. I'm against hobbies. It's just people's way of pretending they are doing things and not being lazy. I'm not lazy. I don't think I have been lazy for a second of my life. So I have no need for a hobby."

"I don't know. I like hobbies. I wish I had more hobbies."

"Like what?"

"Basketball."

"You serious?"

I nodded.

"Let's go play right now."

"No."

"Why not?"

"I'm not in the mood."

"Do you even know how to dribble the ball?"

"Maybe I should get into graphic design as a hobby. Make some cash. I don't need much. I could make a small fraction of what you make and be happy."

He nodded and closed his eyes for a minute.

"I got a really important question, Craig," I said.

He opened his eyes and looked at me like a man on his deathbed.

"Who do you think your hottest ex-girlfriend is?"

"Either Loni or Flora."

"Flora was good. But I like her cousin the most."

"Which cousin?"

"The one I made out with that one time. She was definitely the hottest of all of her cousins."

Craig shook his head.

"No," he said. "Absolutely not."

"Craig, I have superior taste."

"Nope. That is incorrect."

"Everyone knows it's true."

"They just tell you that 'cause they feel bad for you."

"Yeah, for being too awesome. People feel bad that I am so

awesome."

"No."

"Your girlfriends always have droopy eyes."

He gave me a confused and disappointed look.

"I get quality," he said.

"Sure. But with droopy eyes. It's okay though. Your mom and your sister have droopy eyes too. So it's like you were genetically engineered to like droopy eyes."

"I don't like you talking about my family that way."

"Sorry. That was a little out of line."

Craig shook his head.

"Have you seen that girl recently?" I asked.

"Who?"

"Flora's cousin. The one I made out with."

"She's dating someone."

"What's he like?"

"He's gross. He's a gross guy. He looks disgusting."

"What's he like?" I asked.

"Gutted. Has this big fat belly. This poorly managed beard. Dresses like a hobo."

I felt hurt. Craig had pretty much described me.

I rubbed my belly. It had gotten too big. I was a mess. I wanted to feel thin and sprightly. I wanted to feel like Christian Slater. I wanted my clothing to fit well.

"Hey we should go get some Japanese food. I need to start eating healthier. And it would make Bella super happy."

"No, I don't like Jap food. Too shiny."

"What about some Thai food?"

"Don't even know what that is."

"What about Mexican?"

He shook his head.

"Here's the thing," he said. "I don't really like food. I just eat to get fuel. I hope one day there will be a pill that gives us all the nutrients we need."

"Really? That's so depressing."

We heard the front door open and close. His parents were home.

We went up and said hello. They were happy to see me, the more so because I had remembered to take my shoes off. Craig's family hated when you dragged mud through their house.

We sat in the living room on their long leather couches and talked. They told me about the casinos they had been going to. They went to casinos all over the country, not just Vegas and Atlantic City. They went to one in Delaware. And one in Maine. And one in Nebraska. They had chips from these casinos framed on their wall.

At one point Craig went to the bathroom and his mother got up and sat next to me. She leaned her head on my shoulder.

"You think he's okay?" she asked. "I think that Flora girl really hurt him."

"He'll be fine," I promised her. "Neither of us really deal with breakups well."

"I just want him to meet someone nice."

"He will."

"You think so?"

"I do."

Craig came back out and we watched some TV. Soon his father was asleep and his mother was vacuuming.

My cell phone rang. It was Bella.

"Where am I?" she asked.

"Craig's parents' house."

"Oh."

"You wanna come in?"

"No, not really."

I laughed, hung up, and said I had to be going.

"I have to go get my girlfriend," I said.

"Oh, where is she?" she asked.

"In the car."

TWENTY-TWO

BELLA WANTED US to get more exercise. She thought we should go running or get a gym membership. I reminded her that we were staying in the Hamptons and the gyms were way too expensive. Besides, the only kind of exercise I was down for was smoking weed and going for walks. Luckily, she was into that too.

"I love walking at night," I told her one time.

"I like the day better," Bella said. "I like the sun."

We were walking past my friend Max's old house. It looked nice and well cared for. When I was young, it had been a run-down shithole surrounded by unmown grass. It was a greasy place. And dingy. Now it was surrounded by a beautiful garden and I felt sad about that.

"I prefer night. It makes me feel like I'm sneaking around. We used to play ring and run around this neighborhood a lot."

"What's that?" Bella asked.

I explained the game. It was simple. Run up to a house. Ring the doorbell. Run and hide. Then do it again and again until the owner freaks out and starts yelling into the darkness.

"That sounds fun," she said.

"We should do it."

"What do you mean?"

"We should play ring and run right now."

"No, I don't want to."

"Lame. You are making this night lame."

"Am not. Just don't want to get arrested."

"It's such a fun game though."

"Did Craig used to play?" she asked.

"No. He was a good kid. He never really did anything wrong. He didn't even have a crush on a girl until he was like sixteen."

"Maybe he went through puberty late."

"No way. He had so much pubic hair. He looked like a gorilla. A really skinny gorilla."

We headed home. And, as we walked, I continued telling stories about all the mischievous crap we did when I was young. How my buddy used to poop in people's cars. Another buddy peed into jack-o-lanterns. How we would pee into squirt guns and steal our dads' porn. She thought the stories were funny, but I could tell she felt left out. She had not done these things as a child.

"Let's prank Carl," I said.

"That would be fun. Let's not pee on him though."

"No pee. We'll ring and run him."

"Neither of us are good at running."

"It doesn't matter."

When we got home we ran up to the front door, knocked, and ran away. We ran up again and knocked a second time and darted across the lawn to hide in the woods.

We waited.

Then Bella noticed that Carl wasn't home. The house was empty. We had been waiting on nobody. On nothing. We had pranked ourselves.

TWENTY-THREE

THERE WAS A runty redheaded boy named Steven in our program who spent most of his time complaining and pouting or pretending to be a monster. He would make spitty action sounds with his mouth then rip his shirt off and all the girls would tell him he was gross.

None of the parents liked him either. Some took their kids out of the program, insisting that he was a spitter and they didn't want their kids to get diseases. Even my father's secretary, Hilda, seemed to have a vendetta against this little boy.

She confronted me about it after church one Sunday. My father had just given a sermon on porches. He wished people hung out on porches more often. He felt it was a grave sin to spend so much time inside and not on your porch. My dad's new manse had a porch, but I had never actually seen him out there.

Heidi sat me down during coffee hour. We sat at a fold out table and she tried to convince me to kick Steven out of my program.

"Why?" I said. "He's just an annoying kid. He hasn't done anything that bad."

"His father's a crackhead," Hilda said.

"That sucks. I feel bad for him. Why would I kick him out over that?"

"This is just a heads up. The mom's a piece of work too. She sleeps around. Loves drama."

"Everyone loves drama," I said.

"He's a very unstable kid," she said.

"He has poor social skills and he's bratty, but he's really not that bad. He reminds me of myself sometimes."

She gave me a weird look.

"I mean he reminds me of me when I was kid. I could be pretty awkward too, but people just happened to like me."

"I'm just saying," she went on. "He's trouble."

"I'm not kicking him out."

"Fine, but don't say I didn't warn you."

The next day Steven seemed to be doing well. He played on a swing set. He seemed calm and content.

Then he came up to me. He made an angry face.

"I hate this place. I'm going to blow it up," he said.

"Don't say that."

"It's the truth."

"Let's not make terrorist threats, okay? How 'bout you shoot everyone with lava guns or something."

"I hate lava," he said.

"Me too," I admitted.

TWENTY-FOUR

IT GOT HOT. Too hot.

And there were bees. They swarmed around the kids' snacks. Nobody liked the bees, obviously, but Steven seemed especially mad.

"I hate bees," he said.

"We all do," I said.

"My dad kills bees."

"Does he?"

"My dad kills all the bees!"

He looked so mad.

"Go kill some bees then," I said.

"My dad and I both hate bees!"

"That's great," I said.

He growled at me.

I growled back.

He didn't seem impressed.

TWENTY-FIVE

BELLA AND I took the kids to the beach. I was in a foul mood that day. It was too hot and too humid. The beach was crowded. Only a few kids came and Bella took them swimming.

I stayed behind on the sand and tried to read, but the book I brought along wasn't very good.

To pass the time I started building a small structure out of driftwood. It was elaborate and sturdy. I put a gull feather in the center.

The kids found me working and wanted to know what it was.

"I call it Bird Castle," I said.

"Why?" Mandy asked. "So the birds have a place to do you-don't-even-want-to-know-what?"

"I hate birds!" Steven said.

"Shut your fucking dingle face," Mandy said.

Steven growled.

I told everyone to chill out.

I had them walk about ten feet from the fortress and gave them all a handful of beach pebbles.

"Our mission is to destroy Bird Castle."

They liked that. Steven really, really liked it.

"FUCK YOU BIRD CASTLE!" Mandy yelled.

We all chucked our rocks at Bird Castle.

"I hate birds," Steven kept saying.

It was a lot of fun. I got really into it.

"FIRE AT WILL!" I yelled.

Mandy couldn't stop laughing. She loved when I got excited like this.

"Why aren't more adults silly like this?" she asked.

"My dad said he's not a real adult," another kid said.

"Did he?" I asked.

"Are you a real adult?" Mandy asked.

"I guess not."

"Eddie," Steve asked. "Can I throw a really big rock at the castle?"

"Sure."

He found a rock and heaved it, but it was too heavy and it did not reach the Bird Castle.

The kids kept chucking rocks. They did some damage and eventually got bored. The thing was still intact, the feather protected.

"What do we do now?" one of the kids asked.

"We just let it be. We lost. Bird Castle remains undefeated."

"That sucks," Mandy said.

We walked away from the castle and found Bella swimming.

We all held hands and started walking toward the waves.

TWENTY-SIX

STEVEN STOPPED GOING to Fun Squad for a while. Heidi thought I had finally come to my senses and kicked him out. I assured her I had not come to my senses at all. Bella agreed. We were worried about the kid. We wanted him to come back.

A week or so passed and Steven finally came back.

We told him we were happy to see him.

"I hate Fun Squad," he said.

Then he started crying.

He cried the entire day.

"I don't know why you call this Fun Squad," he would yell. "This isn't even fun!"

"It is too fun!" Mandy yelled.

The rest of the kids followed Mandy's lead and ganged up on Steven. They imitated the way he cried and pretended he smelled bad and that the smell made them want to puke.

It was hard to watch.

"We need to talk to them," Bella said. "This is getting way too messed up. I feel like we are running an after school special or something."

I agreed. I got really loud and told them all to shut up. Then I made them all sit in a circle near the slide. I asked them why they were so mad.

"He's a bully," one girl said.

"He's really not," I said.

"Yes he is. My mom says he doesn't get bathed enough and that he is a bully."

"I don't think you kids understand how bullying works. Bullies pick on people. They're not the ones who get picked on. You see, you all are the ones bullying him. Not the other way around."

"Ew," Mandy said.

I could tell I wasn't really getting through to them. They didn't understand what bullying was and that seemed really odd to me. When I was young I got bullied. Bigger kids made fun of me and pushed me into puddles and gave me wedgies and fed me worms and their boogers and stuff like that. It seemed like a simple concept. I had heard that schools were really coming down on bullying, but these kids didn't even know what it was.

Steven became more anti-social. He would spend entire afternoons crying and shadow boxing. He would pretend to be a demon or a monster or a ghost. He started calling himself a karate demon. I thought it was actually a pretty cool idea, and I also thought the crying kinda added to the creepiness of the character.

When the other kids picked on Steven I yelled at them and put them in time out. I even sent one kid home. This did not go over well. The parents became upset and we started losing kids. I liked that. It made the job easier. Watching four kids could barely be considered work, and Bella agreed, but she was concerned about our finances.

"I hate finances," I told her.

PART

TWO

TWENTY-SEVEN

BELLA AND I ran into Craig during one of our walks into town. He wanted us to come drink with him at Chester's, an expensive bar on the wharf, near all the large yachts.

"Fine, but you've got to pay for our drinks," I said.

"Sounds good," he said. "Let's go."

We met his friends from work. Bella tried to interact but they ignored her. Nobody talked much at all. They had their cell phones out and they were either texting or playing games.

The beers were expensive and the service was lousy. Bella kept trying to engage the other people at the table and they ignored her.

Occasionally, they posed for a group picture, a group selfie, and then they looked happy, like they were having the time of their lives. Once the photo was done, they looked bored. They acted like teenagers ignoring their parents.

Craig and I goofed around and drank. He ordered us some shots. We got buzzed.

Bella sat to the side, bored. Eventually she decided to go home. She told me I should stay out and spend some time with Craig. I apologized profusely for being a lousy boyfriend and letting her get bored. She promised me she was fine.

"You're the best," I said

"I really am."

We kissed and she headed out.

Not long after Bella went home, Craig's coworkers also decided to leave. He got mad. He wanted them to stay. He wanted them to party. He yelled at them. At first it sounded like he was joking, like he was just giving them some crap. Then it became obvious he was really upset.

"That's it," he said to them as they got in their cars. "I'm tired of all of you. I'm tired of you all slowing me down. I'm tired of fucking playing T-ball with you losers. Craig is ready for the major leagues. I should be Babe Ruthing all over the place."

"I'm the champ!" he yelled as we walked away from his friends and down Main Street.

A group of attractive women passed by.

"*Angels in the Outfield!*" he called to them.

They laughed and rolled their eyes.

At one point he saw a group of pre-teens on skateboards and offered to give them his autograph.

"You play baseball?" one asked.

"Motherfucker, I am baseball! I'm the champ!"

They didn't have any baseball cards on them, but they let Craig sign their arms and their skateboards.

"I'm a legend!" Craig kept yelling.

I was loving this. I tried to get in on the action. But when I reached over to sign one of the kids' arms he looked at me like he was about to yell "STRANGER DANGER!"

Eventually we headed to Murf's. The bartender asked us what we wanted. I ordered a beer.

"Give me some Pete Rose!" Craig yelled.

The bartender looked confused.

"Daryl Strawberry me, motherfucker!"

"I don't know what that is," the bartender said.

"Give us two Babe Ruths with lime," I said.

Craig put his arm around me. "That's my man. We are champions."

"*League of Their Own!*" I yelled. "Give me some *Field of Dreams*, with lime."

"Eddie, you wild animal!" he said. "I love you."

The bartender was not amused. He reached under the counter and came up with two Bud Lights.

"This will have to do," Craig said.

We sat and drank.

"My team's too minor league these days," he said. "Shit, my team's in diapers. Too much yoga. I don't like it. I need heavy hitters."

"They love their cell phones."

"They're like teenagers. I always have to 'roid up to win the game."

"I don't like them. They're kind of awful."

"I don't really like them either," he said.

"The game has changed. Too much trading teams. I'm not good at this. I'm the type of guy that has one best friend and a girlfriend and a job. That's it. Baseball's too much of a team sport. I need to just do some Olympic shit."

"Like figure skating?"

"No. Not like that. I mean like baseball. But where I'm the only player on the team. Or maybe I could clone myself a bunch of times."

"That could work."

TWENTY-EIGHT

WE HAD A few drinks and were feeling good and lovable. The baseball monologues seemed to be fizzling out for a bit.

Then Craig saw an old friend, a kid he used to play baseball with back in high school. I couldn't believe it. It was as if Craig had conjured the kid up with all his weird baseball talk.

"Ray Goforth?" he said.

A handsome, burly looking man turned and smiled.

"It's me. Craig."

"No shit."

"What's up, dude?"

"You're Craig?"

"Yeah, motherfucker."

"That kid with the giant Adam's apple?"

Craig leaned his head back and made his Adam's apple bob up and down.

"Holy shit!"

The old friends embraced.

Ray sat with us. He and Craig talked about old times, recalling old games and awkward coaches.

Craig ordered us drinks.

They drank hard.

I couldn't keep up. I wanted to. I wanted to feel belligerent and happy, but I didn't have it in me.

The bartender brought me more beer.

Ray walked to the jukebox and turned on some rap. Craig loved rap. He became even more excited.

He started dancing. Craig had moves. He was light on his feet and sassy.

Ray cheered him on.

"That's my good buddy, Craig," he said to me.

TWENTY-NINE

I WENT OUT to smoke a cigarette and called Bella. She didn't answer.

A man walked up to the bushes that lined the outside of the bar. We nodded, acknowledging each other. He took out his sizable penis and began to urinate on the side of the bar. His piss landed about two feet from me, ran down alongside the bar, onto the cement, forming a puddle and then a steady stream.

He finished and walked off with his wiener and balls still hanging out of his pants.

I lit another cigarette. I thought about the night and how I needed to get more into the spirit of things.

I tried to hype myself up. I tried to make myself feel loud inside. To be filled with charm. The sloppiest of charm.

Then I thought about Bella's butt. It seemed so big and

toasty. I felt homesick again. Bella was in my childhood home right now, sleeping, mouth open, drool spilling out and gathering onto my pillow. I thought about making her breakfast in the morning. I could make scrambled eggs. I wasn't a good cook. I made a mess out of everything. But I thought I could manage scrambled eggs. It was easily one of the easiest things to cook next to cereal and orange juice.

The homesickness got worse. I had to stop thinking about breakfast. I had a long night ahead of me. I had to channel my sloppier side. I had to resurrect some of that deep desperate pubic hair energy and carry it into the night like a torch. Maybe I could grab a stranger's butt. I had to get in the mood. That shadow boxing, howling at the street lights, running on fumes, loudly sneaky, foggy-minded, romantic, rabid with ghosts kinda mood. I had to feel the eye of the tiger. I tried to remember if the eye of the tiger was a baseball thing or not, since the theme of the night was obviously baseball.

THIRTY

WHEN I GOT back inside, Craig and Ray were arguing with the bartender. Craig wanted to order three pint glasses full of Hennessy. The bartender did not seem annoyed or even surprised by the strange order. He seemed a little confused. He couldn't tell if my friends were being serious.

Then Craig started throwing twenty-dollar bills at him.

"You like that!" Craig kept yelling. "I got plenty more where that came from!"

The bartender rolled his eyes.

I felt bad for the guy. I remembered being young. Like eighteen or nineteen. He deserved better from us. This dude had fed us drinks even though he was fully aware we were just kids. Now we were grown and acting like bullies.

"Give us what we want!" Craig said.

"Shower him in money, Craig. I want that Hennessy!" Ray

yelled.

The bartender shook his head, told us to relax, then gave Craig three pint glasses full of Hennessy. He and Ray drank it like it was Gatorade. I took a few sips. I didn't like it.

"Drink it down, boys. I got three more glasses on the way!" Craig yelled.

I smiled politely. Then I poured the rest on the ground, secretly. It was late and the bar was packed and sloppy and nobody noticed.

THIRTY-ONE

THERE WAS NO way I could catch up to them while they were drinking pint glasses filled with liquor, but I was starting to feel a bit belligerent and even thinking about dancing and shaking my stuff around. Maybe I'd grab a stranger's butt. A warm butt. But when I danced I just spun around like a chubby tornado. No grace. No rhythm. It barely looked like dancing at all.

Craig liked it though.

"Go Grimboli! Boogie down, you motherfucker!" he yelled.

There were some women there. They were not dancing with me. They were not dancing at all. Nobody was dancing. I wasn't even dancing. Not really. And I liked it this way. I had room. In clubs the dance floors became crowded. They made me claustrophobic. I preferred bars like this. Bars where I could truly stumble around and be sloppy and spin or dance or whatever this was.

Craig didn't like this though. He wanted people to dance. He yelled at people and told them to get rowdy with me.

"You motherfuckers love Grimboli's moves. They make you want to do stuff. But you don't 'cause you are afraid of the magic. Grimboli got that magic. Look at him dance. He's fucking smooth. He's my best buddy and he fucking dances. Why won't any of you fucks dance with him? You're hurting his feelings, you motherfuckers!"

Ray came over and asked Craig if he could borrow money.

Craig howled, threw a bunch of twenties at Ray, then joined me on the dance floor.

Craig had more sophisticated moves. He glided across the sticky floor like he was Jesus walking over water. A couple women danced with him for a bit. But their boyfriends got jealous and pulled them away. Craig started dancing more aggressively.

Ray was also dancing. He had no moves though. He just wobbled to the music and spilled his glass of Hennessey on himself. At one point he stopped and just stood there looking like he was going to puke.

Then he started dancing again. But not in a fun way. He just wobbled back and forth like a kid whose mom had forced him to dance during a wedding.

His face looked uneasy to me. At first he seemed nauseous. Then he looked deep in thought.

He started wandering around.

I saw him walk up to a woman with huge amounts of red hair and dense freckles on her arms and cheeks.

She was beautiful and friendly looking, but Ray looked at her in a sour away. I recognized the look on his face. That look made me think of this greasy doctor I had in college. He was a known quack. He always had this sour look on his face. It was a look that made him seem inept. He had that look on his face when he stuck a Q-Tip up my dick hole. I cursed and screamed and he just laughed. Anyway, Ray had that look on his face now. He had the look of an old and worn-out and mean-spirited doctor.

He tried to joke and flirt. The woman didn't respond. She ignored him. At this point Ray was soaked in Hennessey. He reeked of booze. The woman winced when he got too close. She hated his smell.

Ray kept trying to talk to her.

The woman tried to walk away. But he kept close to her.

Then I saw him sneak up behind her and reach his hand up her skirt, the front not the back.

"Just checking your oil, baby!" he said.

The woman's eyes became as wide as a scream. Her friend lunged at Ray. He grabbed Ray's shirt collar.

"What the fuck you doing, dude?"

The guy slapped Ray.

"I was just . . ." Ray said.

The guy slapped him again.

Craig and I tried to step in, but things felt too sloppy. Too raw and blistered and explosive.

For a moment it looked like the redheaded woman was about to cry.

Her chin was shaking and her eyes stayed wide and hurt.

Then she lunged at Ray.

"Who does that?" she yelled. "What the hell is wrong with you?"

She slapped him.

"Everyone calm down!" Craig yelled.

"You fucking pieces of shit!" one of the women yelled.

"Relax!" Craig yelled. "My buddy just got carried away."

"He grabbed me!" the woman yelled. "I was just trying to have a nice time with my friends and your fucking gross friend fucking grabbed me!"

Craig looked at Ray and me. He was at a loss for words.

The bartender walked up to us.

"You fucking nerds need to get out of here before I call the cops," he said.

"Did he call us nerds?" Craig said.

"Let's just get out of here," I said.

THIRTY-TWO

"COME ON!" CRAIG yelled. "We just need to get to my car. I'll drive you home."

Craig didn't seem as feisty and crazed anymore. He had settled down into the role of supportive coach.

Ray, on the other hand, was wilder than ever. He stumbled away from us, tripped over his own feet, and fell.

He started rolling around.

"Is he trying to roll himself home?" I asked.

"Come on, Ray. My car's close. Pull yourself together, man. The game's over."

"Leave me! I'm going to sleep here!"

"NO!" Craig yelled. "I'M BRINGING YOUR DUMB ASS HOME!"

"I don't even like you that much!" Ray yelled.

We took him by the arms and dragged him down Main

Street. Everything was closed except 7-Eleven but that was on the other side of town.

Ray kept yelling at us. He really didn't want a ride home, but Craig insisted it was his duty to make sure Ray got home safe and sound.

"Shut the fuck up!" a woman yelled from her apartment window. "I'm trying to sleep."

"Fuck you!" Ray yelled.

Another set of apartment lights turned on.

"I'm calling the cops!" a man yelled.

"I'm sorry for waking you!" I yelled back. "We'll be gone soon!"

THIRTY-THREE

WE FINALLY MANAGED to drag Ray to Craig's car, which was parked outside the variety store where Craig used to work when he was a gangly teenager.

We threw him into the back seat. He covered his crotch with his hands.

"I'm not going to fuck you guys!" he yelled.

"What did you say?" Craig asked.

"I don't want to let you guys fuck me!" he yelled. "I won't do it."

Craig reached into the car and grabbed Ray.

"That's it!" Craig yelled. "You piece of shit."

He pulled Ray out of the car and threw him into the middle of Main Street.

Ray got up, stumbled, fell, got up again and managed to stumble to the other side of Main Street.

THIRTY-FOUR

MY HOME WAS only a mile or so away, but I was worried that someone had called the police on us, so I wanted to get home as fast as possible. I missed Bella. I was sure she was at home and her body was warm and she was probably drooling onto my pillow.

So I climbed into Craig's car.

"Let's get the fuck out of here!" I said.

I looked over at him. He still seemed angry. That whole thing with Ray had really gotten to him.

"Take me home, dude," I said. "I'm tired."

Craig shook his head. He looked like he was about to laugh or yell at me. I couldn't tell which.

Then he pulled out of the parking space and started doing doughnuts in the middle of Main Street. The car made nails-on-a-chalkboard screeching sounds.

I looked over at my childhood friend. He had a bratty expression on his face.

"Craig, what the fuck are you doing?" I said.

He drove up onto the curb, then off, and did a few more doughnuts.

"Craig, seriously, stop!"

He shook his head and rolled his eyes at me.

Then he shifted gears and pressed on the gas.

He turned left onto the bridge.

I noticed the speed gauge. By the time we were over the bridge we were going over ninety miles per hour.

I put my seat belt on.

THIRTY-FIVE

I KEPT BEGGING him to slow down.

He didn't respond. His face reminded me of my stepmother's. She wore that same face when she became demanding and stubborn and strong-willed.

I started crying and screaming, begging for him to slow down. I didn't know what had come over him, but I had a feeling we weren't heading to my home. He looked determined. I needed to get out of the car. This terror ride could go on and on. I had a feeling I was going to end up in Brooklyn. Or Iowa.

"FUCKING STOP!" I yelled.

He took a sharp turn.

I felt the car shake. We were off the road.

THIRTY-SIX

THE CAR SPUN and crashed.

Craig looked over at me.

"We have to get out of here," he said.

He pressed on the gas. There was the sound of metal scraping the road.

I unbuckled and ran out of the vehicle.

I wanted to get away from him. He felt like the undertow and the taste of saltwater waves and the casual way the people on the beach look at you, not knowing you are afraid.

THIRTY-SEVEN

I RAN UNTIL I reached a fence. Then I followed the fence, hoping it would lead me somewhere safe.

I heard my name being called.

I followed the sound until I found a woman standing in the road near the car.

"Eddie?"

It was Lisa.

"Hey . . ." I said.

My voice sounded like a child's.

I walked toward her. She had my wallet and my license in her hand.

"You okay?" she asked.

"I was in an accident."

"Jesus fucking Christ."

"I think I'm not too hurt."

THIRTY-EIGHT

SHE TOOK ME to her house across the street. I checked my body. It didn't hurt. It didn't seem like any bones were broken.

I had some tiny pieces of glass sticking out of my fingers and my hand and my head. I plucked the glass out and bled a little.

She wanted to know what had happened.

"So how you doing?" I said. "I haven't seen you in a while."

"Dude, Eddie, what the fuck happened?"

"Craig went nuts," I said.

Her brother and mother came in. He had just checked on the crash. He told us they had found Craig. Apparently he had been looking for me. The cops had come and taken him away.

Lisa gave me a beer and cigarette.

"He went fucking nuts," I kept saying.

THIRTY-NINE

WE STOOD IN her kitchen and smoked cigarettes and drank light beer and talked. I kept going over the crash.

After an hour or so, Lisa drove me home.

We hugged. She looked emotional and kind and familiar.

I walked into the house. I snuck through the kitchen and the dining room and the living room. I woke Bella up.

"Something happened," I said.

She opened her eyes.

"You're bleeding," she said.

"Not badly."

"What the fuck? Eddie, what's going on?"

"I got in a car crash. Nothing's broken though. At least I don't think so."

"Eddie . . ."

She started to cry.

I held her for a while.

She stayed up with me and I went over the accident over and over, just as I had with Lisa.

After an hour or so she started to nod off. I let her sleep.

It was late. Soon the sun would be up. I lay down next to her. I felt her large butt against my leg. Sleep was impossible. Hell, I was having trouble blinking . . .

FORTY

THE NEXT DAY Bella and I went to the site of the crash. There was glass and cans of diet soda and lottery tickets and business cards I had collected over time and pieces of metal on the road. I could see tire marks looping for over a block. The car must have lost control and spun for a while before crashing. That was what had slowed us down from ninety miles per hour to something we could survive.

Being drunk also helped. It kept my body from getting tense and stiff and breaking. I had no broken bones. Just massive warm black bruises on my arms and legs and thighs. Most of my right leg was bruised. It was hard to walk because my body was so swollen and tender.

Craig called that afternoon. I was sitting on the front stoop wearing nothing but my boxers and an unbuttoned shirt.

My hands shook as I put the phone up to my ear. I was

scared. It was a very familiar kind of scared too. It reminded me of when I was little and asked this girl out on a date and knew she didn't like me but I felt like I had to ask anyway. That's what it felt like. I don't know why. But it did.

I could tell he was scared too.

"Grimboli, I'm so sorry," he said.

"It's okay, man."

"I almost killed you."

He told me he was in a blackout. He didn't remember much. He didn't even remember meeting Ray or dragging him to the car or any of that stuff.

"I remember you crying though," he said.

He told me he came to as he was driving us around. He remembered me sitting in the passenger seat crying, then the car spinning out of control. He remembered the spinning. I just remembered the being afraid, the car shaking then hitting something.

The back of the car had hit the tree. That, along with the spinning, had made the impact less brutal.

"You ran into the woods and I chased after you."

"I was afraid," I said.

"Of me?"

"You were acting weird."

"Fuck."

"Did you get hurt?" I asked.

He laughed.

"Yes, but not from the accident. I ran into a tree while I was looking for you. I Wile E. Coyoted and broke my nose."

"That's it? Nothing else?"

"My ankle hurts a little."

"Craig, I'm all bruised up. I look like my stepmother."

He almost laughed.

"I'm so sorry."

"It's okay. We should both be in a body cast or some shit. We lucked out."

FORTY-ONE

I SPENT THE rest of the day in bed. Bella dug up an old TV that had a VHS player and bought me a Stephen King mini-series to watch. It was great. I loved how low-budget and cheesy Stephen King movies were. This one was called *The Storm of the Century*. It took place in a small island town in Maine. There were lots of cheap effects. Lots of fake rain and people dressed like they were from a Sears catalogue from the late nineties. Many of the women dressed like my mom with big baggy sweaters and light blue jeans.

Bella watched some of it with me. But she kept falling asleep. She was exhausted. Usually, when she fell asleep during a movie, I would try and wake her. This time I just let her sleep.

FORTY-TWO

THAT SUNDAY, BELLA and I had to get up and run a fund-raiser out of my father's church for our program. It was a simple event. All I had to do was talk about the kids and what we were doing at Fun Squad. But my body had gotten more messed and tender and swollen and it was hard to even stand. By the time church was done I was exhausted.

During coffee hour I lay on a couch under a portrait of an old minister that had served at the church in the fifties. My kids huddled around me and asked about the accident. I came up with strange lies. I told them I got into a fight with a shark in the ocean. I told them I was secretly a professional football player.

Eventually they became tired of me making up things.

"Tell us the truth!" Mandy said.

"I was in a car accident."

"How?"

"I spun off the road and crashed."

"Are you a really bad driver?"

"The worst," I said.

FORTY-THREE

EVENTUALLY THE KIDS ran off and Bella and I sat on the couch together. I was eating finger food and had my leg propped up on a foldout chair. All the old church ladies were giving me suspicious looks.

"Why don't you just tell them the truth?" she asked.

"'Cause I don't want them to know about my drinking and driving."

"But you weren't the one driving."

"Still, it looks bad."

"I think it already looks bad. I mean, this is a small place. Don't you think they will find out?"

"It's a good point. I mean, they already probably know you're a pothead."

"What do you mean? How would they know that?"

"By the way you act and dress and your overall personality."

She liked that idea at first, but then she started getting insecure.

"I'm responsible though," she said.

"You're not that responsible."

"Neither are you."

We started bickering about who was more responsible. She won the argument. That wasn't hard, though. I had spent years harvesting my inner slacker.

My bruised legs started to really hurt. When I moved them even slightly, they burned so badly I could hardly stand it. One of the old ladies from the church noticed I was in pain. She gave me a pill. I took it. Eventually the pain subsided a bit. I fell asleep. When I woke up I was alone in the church lounge. It felt peaceful at first. Then I got lonely and called out Bella's name. No response.

I stumbled to my dad's office. I dialed her cell from his phone but she didn't pick up. I had a crying jag. It was good and long.

Bella found me weeping. She had brought me pizza for a late lunch.

FORTY-FOUR

AFTER EATING, BELLA and I walked to my father's manse. I could tell he wanted to talk about the accident, but I was too tired.

I took a nap on his couch and when I woke up we watched some movies. He had all the sappy movies I had grown up with. *Fried Green Tomatoes. Legends of the Fall. A League of Their Own.*

We barely got through the opening credits of the first movie before Patty and I started crying.

Bella thought this was hilarious.

"Nothing's even happened yet," she said.

"Oh, you shut up," Patty said.

FORTY-FIVE

WE DIDN'T FINISH the movie. Bella and I got restless.

Even though my body still felt sore and stiff, I could manage to walk. All I wanted to do was walk with Bella and talk.

So we headed back to the church and roamed around the graveyard there.

We smoked a little weed. I felt good. After a night of drinking Hennessy out of a pint glass, weed felt wholesome, like drinking hot cocoa or milk and cookies.

"What do you think is going to happen to Craig?" Bella asked.

"Don't know."

"He's probably in some legal trouble."

"He's going to get his license taken away," I said. "There will be tons of fines and stuff like that."

"Are you mad at him?"

"No."

"Not at all?"

"Nope."

"That's kinda weird. I'm mad at him."

"You shouldn't be."

"Don't tell me how to feel."

"I'm not."

"Yes you are."

"Listen, I knew what I was doing getting in that car with him. You know, when he first got his license he liked to drive like a fucking lunatic. One day we drove up to the Smith Haven Mall because he wanted to buy video games. He was a complete nerd. All he wanted to do was play video games. He drove so fast. And I loved it. I never felt afraid. Driving around with Craig like that used to be one of my favorite things. Last summer Craig and I went to this club and on the way home he went over a hundred miles per hour. I didn't even know his car could go that fast."

"And you weren't scared?"

"No. I loved it. I was laughing and cheering him on and shit."

She looked sad.

"This was not the first time we had driven around like that," I told her. "This was the first time I was scared. Man, I used to think it was so much fun. He drove down the back roads, getting that shitty car to go almost a hundred and I would just howl and kick my legs around, loving every minute of it."

My legs started to hurt. I sat on a grave.

"I don't know why I was so scared this time," I said.

"Because you got into an accident. You almost got killed."

"I didn't know that was going to happen. But I was scared anyway."

"I don't think that's a bad thing."

"I do."

FORTY-SIX

BELLA WAS WORN out. Seeing me bruised and moaning and limping around made her anxious and watching sappy movies didn't help her. They just wore her out further.

She wanted to meet up with Robin and go to a yoga class. Usually I ranted about how much I hated yoga. Yoga made the butts go away. I hated it. And I could be very loud about it. That afternoon, I was too tired for all that. I told her to go.

"You just going to watch sappy movies all day again?"

"All day, every day."

Things didn't work out as I had planned though. Patty was watching her soaps and, even though she was asleep more than half the time, she would not let us watch anything else. I tried to get into her soaps with her, but it was too confusing.

I was bored. I missed Bella. I regretted not going with her. I mean, there was no way I could do yoga. Even when I was well, yoga seemed impossible to me. Now that I was bruised up like this, yoga seemed like torture. Still, I wished I was there. I wanted it so badly I almost started to cry. But I held it back.

Home was far away. It was three miles to the ferry. Then another two to get home. God only knew how far away the yoga studio was. But I figured by the time I got home, yoga would be over and we could smoke weed and walk around and feel goofy together.

So I got up and kissed Patty on the forehead as she slept.

I stumbled out the door and headed down the road and started walking home.

Eventually I realized I could have asked my dad for a ride. But at that point I had already walked a mile or so. I felt flaky to the core. Maybe I had brain damage or something. I kinda remembered hitting my head during the accident. For a moment it all seemed really funny. Then my legs started to really hurt. I sat on the side of the road and watched fancy cars drive by.

It was warm. I considered napping.

Then, on a whim, I stuck my thumb out. I had never hitch-hiked before. I had always been a little paranoid about being kidnapped, but I wasn't a kid anymore. Anyway, did that even matter? Adults got kidnapped too. Maybe there was some rich perv out there who liked hand jobs from bruised up fat dudes.

A car slowed down but only for a moment.

"Nice pants!" a young man yelled from his window.

I looked down and saw a hole in the crotch of my slacks. I felt around. There were no underpants. Just balls. Big balls.

I kept my thumb out until a beat up Volkswagen pulled over.

I got up and staggered over. The driver was a thirty-year-old Mexican woman with a trusting smile.

I thanked her for the ride and even paid for our ferry ride over.

"I don't usually hitchhike," I said. "My parents made me all paranoid. They convinced me that if I did, I would end up getting kidnapped and molested in a dungeon. Now I hitchhike and I get picked up by you, and can you even imagine wanting to, you know, put me in a basement and do stuff to me?"

"Stuff?"

"You know, like fingering me and stuff."

"I don't know."

"I'm just saying it's important to trust people."

"Right."

I saw my road and told her to turn right. She shook her head and pulled over.

"Can you walk from here?"

I nodded and got out.

I waved to her as she drove off.

FORTY-SEVEN

THAT NIGHT CARL made us prime rib and we ate and got stuffed. Usually we would spend the rest of the night watching sitcoms and trying to laugh ourselves back to life, but Robin didn't like being so inactive. She wanted to go for a walk. Bella liked that idea.

We headed down to the beach and sat on the sand. My legs hurt. Bella suggested I swim in the cold bay.

The dark waves looked refreshing. Even the sound the water made on the sand seemed to soothe my muscles.

I got up and took my pants off. This was immediately problematic. I still had no underpants on.

"Holy shit!" Bella yelled. "Release the twins!"

"Who are the twins?" Carl asked.

"The balls!" she yelled.

She laughed.

I worried that I had offended Robin, but then she got up

and took her own clothing off. For a moment I saw a bunch of nakedness and it was a happy and crazed thing.

We ran into the water.

I dove in, enjoying the way the water felt on my butt crack.

Once my lungs hurt I came back up.

Carl had followed us in.

"Are you naked?" I asked.

He nodded.

"Dude, I have never seen you naked before. Jump up and let me see that long cock of yours."

"I don't think so."

"Come on!"

"SHOW US YOUR DICK!" Bella yelled.

"I got a better idea," Robin said. "Let's play chicken."

Bella got on my shoulders and Robin got on Carl's. I found my balance. We were supposed to approach each other and have the girls grapple with each other until one couple fell. The couple still standing would be the winner.

But I started trying to circle around Carl and approach from behind, so I could see Robin's butt. Carl saw me and started to turn. I started running, desperate to see a new butt. I moved too recklessly though, and before I got to see anything I lost my balance and fell into the water.

I liked the feeling of being underwater. I would have hung out there for longer, but my body floated back up to the surface, where I found Bella laughing.

Justin Grimbol has lived in Vermont a bunch of times but will always be from Long Island.

Other **Atlatl Press** Books

Fuck Happiness by Kirk Jones
Impossible Driveways by Justin Grimbol
Giraffe Carcass by J. Peter W.
Shining the Light by A.S. Coomer
Failure As a Way of Life by Andersen Prunty
Hold for Release Until the End of the World
by C.V. Hunt
Die Empty by Kirk Jones
Mud Season by Justin Grimbol
Death Metal Epic (Book Two: Goat Song Sacrifice)
by Dean Swinford
Come Home, We Love You Still by Justin Grimbol
We Did Everything Wrong by C.V. Hunt
Squirm With Me by Andersen Prunty
Hard Bodies by Justin Grimbol
Arafat Mountain by Mike Kleine
Drinking Until Morning by Justin Grimbol
Thanks For Ruining My Life by C.V. Hunt
Death Metal Epic (Book One: The Inverted Katabasis)
by Dean Swinford
Fill the Grand Canyon and Live Forever by Andersen Prunty
Mastodon Farm by Mike Kleine
Fuckness by Andersen Prunty
Losing the Light by Brian Cartwright
They Had Goat Heads by D. Harlan Wilson
The Beard by Andersen Prunty

www.ingramcontent.com/pod-product-compliance
Lightning Source LLC
Chambersburg PA
CBHW050320200626
46812CB00019BA/2814